THE LAST SUPER

CASE FILES: POCKET-SIZED MURDER
MYSTERIES

RACHEL AMPHLETT

SAXON
PUBLISHING

THE LAST SUPER

CHAPTER ONE

Seventeen years, nine months and four days.

And it would all be over within the next five hours.

Larry Patrick raised his chin, straightened his tie, then patted his pockets.

Wallet, keys, cellphone.

He ran his eyes over the cardboard cartons lining the living room wall, taped shut and ready to go. Books, some vinyl records – Lou Reed, Pink Floyd, all the good stuff from the seventies – crockery and clothes.

Dust motes floated in the air and caught the morning sunlight that always struck the front window – never enough to warm the ground-floor apartment, but sufficient to provide a hint of the temperature outside.

The new RV Carol and Gary Petersen had bought with their share of the developer's settlement stood was parked out front.

Thirty-three feet long, sleek, modern.

It took Gary four attempts to shuffle the monstrosity into a tight space between an ancient blue Civic and a Korean-made coupé Larry didn't know the name of, with Carol's attempts to guide her husband not boding well for their impending trip to Florida.

Any other time, there would have been an uproar out there. Someone would complain that it was blocking their view.

Except that the brownstones over the road were boarded up, abandoned these past three weeks.

Even the one painted a peachy hue that always reminded him of the desert at sunset.

An array of trash fluttered against its front stoop as if trying to climb up and seek out a new home beyond the peeling paintwork of the front door, the one with a new padlock fitted to its rusting handle.

Larry lowered his gaze and wondered if he should change out of his monogrammed shirt and into something more casual.

It wasn't as if he would be the building supervisor for much longer.

He huffed under his breath, straightened his shoulders.

No, he would wear it. After all, he still had a job to do, didn't he?

Even if it was only for the next five hours.

Back in 2001, it was all the work he could get.

Too old to go and fight again.

Too young to retire.

Until now.

Rebecca, his daughter, had persuaded him to move closer to her and her husband. A new condo development in Virginia Beach, only a mile or so from where they lived with his two grandkids.

He frowned as he ran his thumb over a piece of tape on one of the cartons, ironing out the creases.

As soon as Bec and David heard the final contracts were signed on the redevelopment, they insisted he move away from the city and, despite the payout he got from the developers, he couldn't afford Virginia Beach on his own.

He argued with them for a time.

He didn't win.

His daughter pointed out that since her mom had walked out on them both eighteen years ago, she owed him.

For the food he put on the table every night.

For the education that got her through college and into university.

For everything.

Now, she was paying him back.

It was because of their idea, their offer of kindness to pay the difference that David was turning up tomorrow with the U-Haul truck to drive him down the coast as the developers began to rip apart his home.

Larry exhaled and moved to the door, his hand shaking as he reached for the handle.

How was he going to tell them that he couldn't leave Baltimore?

CHAPTER TWO

Out in the hallway, his stomach growled as charcoal smoke wafted in through the back door, the promise of grilled steak and a cold light beer tempered with the realization this would be the last time.

The last time they all met up like this to share a meal, catch up with the news, check in on each other.

Would the tenants of the newly refurbished apartments do this in eight months' time when the project was finished?

He wouldn't bet on it.

'Larry!'

He turned at the sound of a cigarette-damaged croak that barked off the walls.

Brenda Friedman, seventy years old – plus a half-decade more by his reckoning – beckoned to him, then handed him a plate of bread rolls and winked.

'Make yourself useful. One each for everyone to start with, plus a burger. There's relish on the table out there, and paper napkins if anyone wants them.'

'Yes, ma'am.' He turned at the sound of an indignant meow to see a large tabby cat peering out from behind the wire mesh door of a kitty carrier. 'You've already packed him?'

'Cats,' said Brenda, and shrugged. 'You know what they're like. They pick up on everything. He'll run and hide if I don't make sure he's somewhere safe.'

'True.' He lowered his voice. 'Any news?'

She shrugged. 'Not a peep. Tried his email last week – that came back undelivered, just like the letter I mailed him three weeks ago.'

'What about that phone number you had for him?'

'I keep leaving messages, but he doesn't call.' She sighed. 'Maybe he just doesn't want to talk to me.'

'Joshua's your son, Brenda.' He reached out and squeezed her arm. 'I'm sure he will, eventually. Don't give up on him.'

'He did time in prison for armed robbery, Larry. I'm the only one who hasn't given up on him.' She patted his hand. 'Don't forget to come get the fruit punch when you're done with the bread.'

CHAPTER THREE

'Hey, Supe.'

Larry paused at the top of the four stone steps to the yard where his neighbors gathered on an uneven patio and grinned as Scott Bancroft raised a bottle of beer in his direction.

'Got you one of these – where've you been?'

'Just checking on a few things.' Careful he didn't trip over one of the cracked and uneven pavers, he crossed to where two trestles had been set out with tablecloths that flapped in a gentle breeze and put the plate of bread rolls beside the relish. 'Water, gas, that sort of thing.'

'It's your last day – take a minute to relax.' Melissa Bancroft called from where she stood beside the smoking grill with a set of tongs in one hand and a glass of iced tea in the other, skin-tight jeans leading up to a Lycra top that clung in all the right places.

Larry smiled. 'Make sure you rehydrate plenty – Brenda's made fruit punch.'

'Thanks for the warning.' Scott handed him the

beer, then turned to watch as two kids screamed with laughter. 'Thanks for sorting out the slip 'n' slide for the grandkids, too.'

'That was Brenda. Said we couldn't have a summer cookout without one.'

'She's right about that. At least it'll keep 'em occupied for a while.'

'When is your son getting here?'

Scott grimaced. 'Later, he says. A last-minute meeting with the divorce lawyer.'

'Sorry to hear that.'

'It's his own fault. Wait until you meet his girlfriend.'

Melissa handed the tongs to Gary Petersen and wandered over. 'Larry, in case we don't get the chance later Scott and I wanted to thank you for everything you've done for us over the years.'

He could feel the heat flushing up across his neck towards his jaw and cleared this throat. 'Only doing my job, ma'am. That's all anyone would do in the same position.'

A heavy hand on his shoulder sent a shudder through his spine.

'Don't be so humble,' said Scott, and handed him an envelope. He shrugged, a ripple of muscles flowing across his broad arms. 'A gift, from us. Open it later if you like.'

'You've worked all hours,' added Melissa. 'Every day. We've been here twelve years, Larry and you've always been there for us – and our kids, when they were home.'

He blinked, took the envelope.

Felt the notes inside.

Folded it and shoved it in his back pocket.

'Thank you,' he murmured.

Another slap on the shoulder.

'Larry – fruit punch!'

'I'd best go get that.'

CHAPTER FOUR

'It feels strange, doing this on a Thursday.'

Carol sat on the bottom step, smiling at a peal of laughter as her granddaughter shot along the slip 'n' slide. 'Instead of our usual Friday, I mean.'

'I don't think it'd be a good idea to try and have a cookout while the place is being torn apart tomorrow,' said Melissa, her words slurring from the potent cocktail in her hand. 'Dust in the food, for starters.'

They sat around the table under a lone silver maple, the roar and crunch of construction work in the next block over echoing across the rooftops.

Larry said nothing, leaned forward and fanned a napkin over the remains of the salad, dispersing the flies that gathered near a pool of olive oil dressing.

'Mom, maybe you should have a glass of water.'

Stuart Bancroft scowled, his expensive suit crumpled as he passed a paper plate laden with food to the skinny brunette twenty-something who hovered at his elbow.

Larry had already forgotten her name.

'I'm fine,' Melissa gurgled. 'Besides, it's our last time here. Lemme enjoy myself.'

The twenty-something blushed and turned away from her boyfriend and his mother, wandering toward the two kids while she picked at her food.

'Always thought they'd carry me out of here in a box,' said Larry, suppressing a belch as he leaned back in his camp chair. 'Didn't expect to have to move at my age.'

'Me either,' said Brenda, then screeched as a spray of cold water hit them.

'Richie, no!'

Stuart shot off toward the kids, snatched the hosepipe from his son and switched off the faucet as both children burst into tears.

'Oh, my.' Brenda took the towel Carol handed over and wiped at the back of her neck. 'It's all right – it doesn't matter. He didn't mean it.'

'I'm so sorry.' Stuart returned to the table, his face puce. 'It's the divorce. They used to be better behaved.'

Larry took the towel and dabbed at his face. 'No harm meant, I'm sure.'

'Mom – we need to make a move. Sorry, but the babysitter's got a date tonight and we're already running late.'

Melinda raised her hands and sighed. 'Looks like the party's over, folks.'

CHAPTER FIVE

The departure of the Bancrofts with their son and grandkids broke up the party, as Melissa predicted.

After tidying away the grill – it was headed to Virginia with Larry – and fetching the last of their belongings from their apartment on the second floor, Carol and Gary climbed into their RV.

'I didn't realize you were leaving tonight as well,' said Brenda, dabbing a tissue to her eyes.

'It's why Gary didn't drink much,' Carol hiccupped.

Her husband smiled, leaning his elbow out of the window and starting to looking comfortable behind the wheel. 'Figured we'd miss some of the traffic – Fridays can be hell on the 95.'

'It's always hell on the 95,' said Larry. He held up his hand. 'Safe travels.'

'Get yourself on social media,' said Carol. 'We'll be sharing the trip as we go.'

'I'll think about it.'

He wandered into the road as Gary started the engine, a soft roar emanating from the engine while he waved them out from the tight space, ignoring the frustrated glare from a delivery driver.

Moments later, they were off, hands waving out the windows as the RV purred away, and Larry returned to the curb outside the brownstone.

'I give them six weeks.'

He smiled as Brenda coughed out a snort, her gaze on the departing vehicle.

'Maybe four,' she said.

'You never know, might be what they needed.'

She laughed as a car pulled into the free space and waved to the driver. 'That's my friend, Dorothy. She lives at the retirement place.'

'That's good to have someone you know there to help you get settled. I'll fetch your bags. When are your cartons being collected?'

'Tomorrow, at eight. I spoke to a woman at the developer's office this morning and she's going to come down here and make sure everything's okay.' Brenda narrowed her eyes. 'Wouldn't want anything stolen.'

'Good thinking. I'll keep an eye on them until then.'

Larry hefted the two large suitcases into the back of the compact, placed the kitty carrier on the rear seat and wrapped the seat belt around it.

The cat mewed at him through the wire door, its eyes wide in confusion.

'Don't worry – I'll put butter on his paws,' said Brenda. 'He'll be fine.'

'I'm sure he will.' Larry shut the door, then helped her round to the passenger side as her friend climbed back behind the wheel. 'You behave yourself, Mrs Friedman. Don't start a riot the minute you get there, you hear me?'

'They have poker games on Friday nights,' she said, her eyes sparkling.

'You'll whip the lot of 'em.' He smiled. 'I'm sure your son will be in touch, too. In his own time. I guess he has a lot of things to process at the moment, having his freedom again after fifteen years.'

She paused, her hand on top of the door. 'I'm going to miss you, Larry.'

'Just doing my job, Mrs Friedman.'

She leaned over and kissed his cheek. 'You've been a good friend. Thank you.'

He waved until Dorothy's car disappeared from sight, then wandered up the four steps to the front door, closing it behind him.

The late summer sun cast a glow across the floorboards, the surface pitted and pockmarked from centuries of foot traffic.

He peered up the staircase.

Instead of voices, music and laughter, the building was silent, dead, except for the sound of his own breathing, his heartbeat in his ears as his gaze fell to the door leading down to the basement.

He blinked, attempting to lose some of the lightheadedness from the beer and Brenda's fruit punch and rummaged in his pocket for his keys.

Unlocking the door, he flipped on the light switch and edged down the stone staircase, careful to keep his hand on the plaster wall.

There was no railing, no way to stop his fall if he slipped.

He shivered when he reached the bottom of the

stairs and stared at the large furnace in the far corner, its huge frame silent and sulking.

He would miss waking to the noise of the heating system coming to life. Six o'clock, every morning without fail in time for his neighbors – his friends – to have hot water and warmth.

Above his head, pipework crisscrossed the low ceiling under his apartment.

It was why he suggested the basement in the first place.

No-one else came down here but the building supervisor.

No-one else would hear.

Larry's gaze roamed to a patch of pale-colored concrete in the floor, uneven with a rough finish, about five feet by two.

Back-breaking work.

When Brenda's son Joshua hammered on his door all those years ago, he knew something was wrong the minute he'd seen the teenager's face.

He wondered, later, whether Joshua inherited his vicious streak from his father but that night...

That night, none of it mattered.

That night, Joshua decided enough was enough.

Old man Friedman used to beat Brenda so hard she wouldn't be seen for days – and she still had bruises when she emerged from the apartment, skittish as a mouse.

She refused to report him, and back then there wasn't much support for victims of domestic violence.

Joshua waited until his mother had locked

herself in the bathroom after another attack, then turned on his dad.

Blind rage turned to panic.

Rebecca was only seven at the time and staying with her paternal grandparents in Brooklyn for the weekend, so she never knew.

Never knew that her father had listened to Joshua's gasping explanation, crossed the hallway and helped the teenager drag his father's body down the basement stairs before his mother realized what happened.

When Brenda emerged from the bathroom an hour later, Joshua said he had told his father to leave, and that he would take care of her.

Which went fine until Joshua killed another man in an armed robbery two years later.

Larry circled the pale concrete rectangle, sweat patches under his arms.

They spent two days chipping away at the floor, away from prying eyes and ears while the neighbors were at work.

On day three, Joshua shoved his father's body into the shallow cavity.

On day four, Larry mixed concrete.

Now the place was going to be redeveloped.

Stripped apart, piece by piece, including the basement.

Where old Harry Friedman lay rotting.

Larry wandered back up the stairs, his tread as heavy as the thoughts that tumbled over in his mind.

Reaching his apartment, he rummaged through one of the boxes before pulling out a half-full bottle of Jameson's and a tumbler, pouring a generous measure with shaking hands.

He moved to the window, took a sip.

Fished out his cellphone.

Stared at the screen.

If Joshua went back to prison before Brenda got the chance to see him again, it would kill her, of that he was sure. There would be no early release for good behavior like last time, no hope of parole – not within Brenda's lifetime.

He topped up the whiskey, squared his shoulders then dialed 911, clearing his throat as the operator answered.

'I'd like to report a homicide. I killed a man.'

Ending the call a few seconds later, Larry turned the tumbler of whiskey in his hand and raised a silent toast to the empty street beyond the window.

Seventeen years, nine months and four days.

He might be the last super, but he looked after his tenants.

THE END

ABOUT THE AUTHOR

Rachel Amphlett is a USA Today bestselling author of crime fiction and spy thrillers, many of which have been translated worldwide.

Her novels are available in eBook, print, and audiobook formats from libraries and retailers as well as her website shop.

A keen traveller, Rachel has both Australian and British citizenship.

Find out more about Rachel's books at: www. rachelamphlett.com.

ALSO AVAILABLE IN THE CASE FILES
SERIES

Nowhere to Run

When a series of vicious attacks leaves the local running
community in shock and fear, probationary detective
Kay Hunter is thrust into the middle of a fraught
investigation.

ISBN eBook: 978-1-913498-68-9

ISBN paperback: 978-1-913498-69-6

Blood on Snow

A suburban housewife is found dead in her garden. There is no weapon, no witnesses, and the only set of footprints belong to her cat.

Probationary detective Kay Hunter and her colleagues are convinced it's murder – but how can they find a killer when there are no clues?

ISBN eBook: 978-1-913498-70-2
ISBN paperback: 978-1-913498-71-9

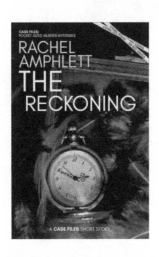

The Reckoning

The newest arrival at a care home for the elderly
carries an air of mystery that even an ex-WW2
Resistance fighter can't help trying to solve.

Then matters take a sinister turn…

ISBN eBook: 978-1-913498-70-2
ISBN paperback: 978-1-913498-71-9

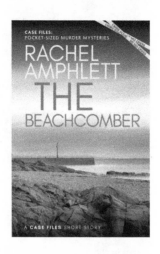

Staying at a tiny guesthouse in Cornwall after the
summer, Julie spends her days combing the
beaches, looking for things to collect while hiding
from her past.

Then a storm breaks, and suddenly she's
scared.

**Because you never know what might wash up
after a storm...**

ISBN eBook: 978-1-913498-93-1
ISBN paperback: 978-1-913498-94-8

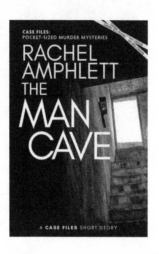

The Man Cave

When Darren regains consciousness in a dank basement, escape turns out to be the least of his worries...

ISBN eBook: 978-1-913498-96-2
ISBN paperback: 978-1-913498-97-9

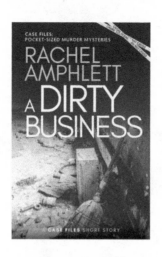

A Dirty Business

When Michael arrives at work early one winter's
day, he discovers that he's not the only one who's
had a busy morning...

ISBN eBook: 978-1-913498-98-6
ISBN paperback: 978-1-913498-99-3

CPSIA information can be obtained
at www.ICGtesting.com
Printed in the USA
BVHW060956090522
636520BV00006B/244

9 781915 231413